Scooby-Dooby-Doo's DOUBLE READER

Written by Gail Herman
Illustrated by Duendes del Sur

ISBN-10: 0-545-00115-3
ISBN-13: 978-0-545-00115-1

Compilation Copyright © 2007 by Hanna-Barbera.
Scooby-Doo Reader #6: The Mixed-Up Museum © 2001 by Hanna-Barbera
Scooby-Doo Reader #14: Football Fright © 2002 by Hanna-Barbera
SCOOBY-DOO and all related characters and elements are trademarks of and © Hanna-Barbera.

Published by Scholastic Inc. All rights reserved. SCHOLASTIC and associated logos are trademarks and/or registered trademarks of Scholastic Inc.

12 11 10 9 8 7 6 5 4 3   9 10/0
Printed in the U.S.A.
First printing, September 2007

SCHOLASTIC INC.
New York Toronto London Auckland Sydney
Mexico City New Delhi Hong Kong Buenos Aires

The Mystery Machine squealed to a stop. Velma jumped out. "We are late!" she cried. "The Museum of Natural History will close before we get to see the dinosaurs."

"Scoob and I are sorry, Velma," Shaggy said. "But like, we *had* to stop for pizza."

"Don't worry, Velma," Daphne said. "There is time to see the new show."

Fred looked at a map. "The Great Dinosaur Hall is this way!"

"But the cafeteria is the other way!" said Shaggy.

Velma led the gang through the
jungle room. Shaggy read a sign.
"Gorillas in the Wild."

"Ratch out!" Scooby shouted. A
gorilla was swinging right at them!

"Don't worry," said Velma. "These gorillas are puppets. They are wired to move and make noise so we can see how they live in a real jungle."

Shaggy sighed. "Like, I wish those bananas were real."

Next they came to the elephants. The animals raised their trunks. "Rakes?" asked Scooby. "Fakes!" said Velma.

"Even those peanuts!" said Shaggy.

Finally, they reached the Dinosaur Hall.
Large dinosaur skeletons peered down at
them. A crowd of people oohed and ahhed.

"Look at that!" Velma said. "A real brachiosaur skeleton!"

"Amazing!" said Fred.

"Jeepers!" said Daphne.

"Rikes!" said Scooby.

The brachiosaur looked too real. Its great jaws opened and closed. "I am starving," Shaggy said.

"Re roo," said Scooby, licking his lips.

Shaggy turned to a security guard. "Like, where's the best place to chow down?" he asked. "The cafeteria is this way," the guard said. He waved his arm, and hit a sign.

"Oops!" said the guard. "I have new glasses. And I still can't see very well. But I can take you to the cafeteria. I have to go that way to start closing the museum."

A few minutes later, Shaggy and Scooby
had emptied the salad bar, the soda
machines, and everything in between.

All at once, the cafeteria lights flickered.
On, off.
On, off.
Shouts echoed all around. Something
was happening!

"Come on, Scoob!" shouted Shaggy.
"We have to find the others!"

They raced back to the Dinosaur Hall. The brachiosaur skeleton swung its mighty head. It snapped its jaws. One leg moved, then another. "It is alive!" a boy shouted.

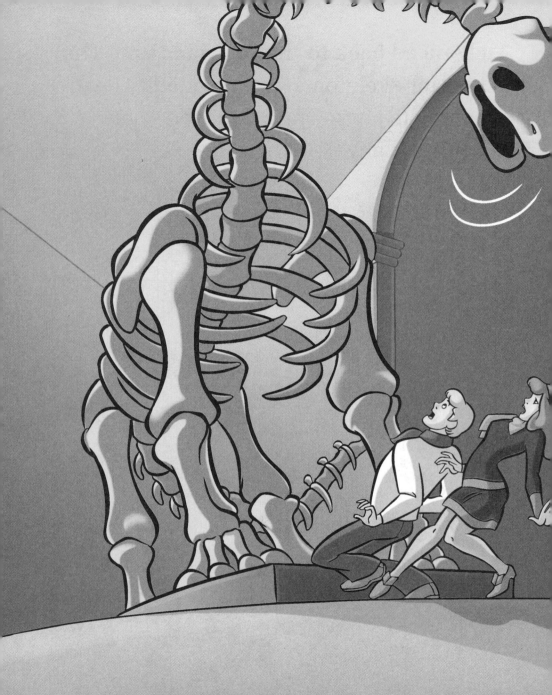

Everyone ran in fright.
"Don't panic!" Velma called.

A shadow fell over the gang. The
dinosaur roared, right over their heads.
"Run!" Fred said.

They raced past the elephants. The
elephants raised their trunks and stomped
their feet. They sounded angry.

Scooby and the gang sped past the gorillas.
The gorillas were swinging from vine to vine.

"It looks like we have a mystery to solve," said Fred.

"But we can't hang around," said Shaggy. "It is closing time."

"Ret's ro!" Scooby agreed.

"Hmm," said Daphne. "Would you stay for a Scooby Snack?"

Awhooo! Howling filled the hall.

"Rikes!" cried Scooby, "a ronster." He jumped into Shaggy's arms.

"How about *two* Scooby Snacks?" asked Velma.

"Rokay!"

"Great," said Velma.

"Now, let's split up and look for clues," said Fred. "Daphne, Velma, and I will find the security guard. He might know something."

Scooby and Shaggy headed down a long, dark hall. With every footstep, they heard strange animal sounds. Then they heard a low, loud moan coming from behind a door.

A sign on the door read KEEP OUT!

"Zoinks! It is a scary jungle beast!"
Shaggy yelped.

"Ruh-roh!" Scooby barked. They raced
back the other way. They crashed right into
Velma, Fred, and Daphne.

Shaggy said, "There's a monster behind
that door! The sign says KEEP OUT! And, like,
that's what I want to do!"

"I have an idea," Velma said.

She flung open the door. Then she flipped on the light.

"Thank goodness!" said a voice.

"Hey, it's the security guard," said Shaggy. "What are you doing here?"

The guard waved around the room. The gang saw buttons and levers and switches. "This is the museum control room," he explained.

"I thought so," said Velma. "I bet you stepped inside to close down the museum. But you could not see very well."

"I turned off the lights by accident," said the guard. "And when I tried to find the switch, I pressed all the wrong buttons."

"And everything went crazy!" Velma finished.
With some help from the gang, the guard quickly
fixed everything. The museum grew quiet.

Then came a long, loud rumbling sound. Everyone jumped. "That's just Scooby's tummy!" said Shaggy. "Hey, can you flip one switch back on? The one for the cafeteria?" "Scooby Dooby Doo!" barked Scooby.

The gang was riding around the parking lot at Coolsville High School. It was the day of the big football game. The parking lot was packed.

Fred, Velma, and Daphne looked for a
parking space.

Zzzzz.

In the back seat, Shaggy and Scooby
snored.

"There are no parking spaces!" Fred said.

Velma nodded. "Fans have been here for hours!" she said.

"Go! Go!" A roar swept over the van.

"And everyone's been shouting for hours," Daphne added.

Just then a loud buzzer sounded. "The game is starting!" said Fred. Shaggy and Scooby were suddenly wide-awake.

"We have to hurry!" Shaggy cried.
He and Scooby raced out of the van.
"We have to get to the snack stand!"

A few minutes later, Shaggy and Scooby
stood in line.

"What do you say, good buddy," Shaggy
said. "Hot dogs with the works?"

"Rulp!" Scooby gulped.

"Yeah, I'm hungry, too," Shaggy agreed.

Scooby shook his head. He pointed to the front of the line.

"Gulp!" Shaggy stared.

A strange-looking creature stared back. Then it disappeared.

"Like, what should we do?" asked Shaggy.
"Reat!" said Scooby.
"Right," Shaggy agreed. "Let's eat."

Chomp! Chomp! Shaggy and Scooby tried
to eat and carry their food at the same time.

"Hey! Let's get a Coolsville High
backpack!" said Shaggy. "We can stash the
grub in there!"

"Rrrrr, rrrrr, grrrrr." Strange voices filled the air.

Two more creatures stepped close to Shaggy and Scooby.

They were orange. Striped. And muttering in a crazy language.

"They're shaped like people," Shaggy whispered. "But they can't be people."

"Raliens!" cried Scooby.

"Aliens!" cried Shaggy.

They dropped their food and ran.

They didn't get far. "Ruh-uh!" said Scooby.
He pointed to the sky.
    "Zoinks!" Shaggy gasped, staring at the sky.

High above them hovered a spaceship.
An alien spaceship!

"Quick!" Shaggy pointed across the field. "Let's find the gang."

The buddies stumbled through the stands. All at once, Scooby stopped. "Rore raliens!"

More aliens streamed through the aisles.
"Rrrrr, grrrr, rrrrr." The strange voices
grew louder.
"RRRRR, GRRRR!" And louder.

"The aliens are taking over!" Shaggy cried. He and Scooby leaped onto the football field. "Everyone! Follow us!"

Plop! A football dropped into
Shaggy's hands. He looked to his right.
More aliens were coming. Bigger,
stronger ones. He looked to his left.
Still more aliens!

Shaggy took off, straight down the
center of the field.
　Scooby's legs spun like wheels as
he tried to keep up.
　Crash! Boom! Aliens fell like
bowling pins.

The buddies raced to the end of the field.
They dove under the goalpost.

"Rouchdown!" shouted Scooby.

A crowd of aliens swooped down. Shaggy
shook them off. "Like, what do you want?"
he cried.

"RRRRR! GRRRR! RRRRR!"

Shaggy didn't know what to do. So he tossed the football.

"Rrrrr! Grrrr!" One alien scooped it up. Then, in a flash, all the aliens raced away.

Shaggy and Scooby found the rest of the gang.

"It's weird, man," Shaggy told the others. "All the aliens wanted was a football. And now they're going back to their spaceship."

"Aliens?" Velma repeated. "Spaceship?" She looked up at the sky. "That's a blimp," she told Shaggy and Scooby. "The kind you see at football games."

"Call it what you want, Velma," Shaggy told her. "But all these orange-and-black spacemen need to get home somehow!"

"Those aren't aliens." Velma shook her head. "Those are fans wearing face paint. Orange and black to look like tigers. For the Terrytown Tigers football team. And some are football players in uniform."

"But what about the strange noises? Rrrrr? Grrrr?" Shaggy asked.

"That's the Tigers' cheer!" said Fred.

"Their voices sound funny from shouting so much!" Daphne added.

Shaggy's face fell. "And to think!" he moaned. "We dropped all that food when we ran away!"

Just then the Coolsville coach walked over.

"Good job carrying the ball, boys," the coach told Scooby and Shaggy. "You really had those Tigers going. Do you want Coolsville jackets? Caps? A team football?"

Scooby and Shaggy shook their heads.
"How about a team dinner?" said Shaggy.
"Scooby-Dooby-Doo!" barked Scooby